THE JUNIOR NOVEL

Adapted by N. B. Grace

Based on the screenplay written by Dan Berendsen

Based on characters created by Michael Poryes and Rich Correll & Barry O'Brien

Executive Producers Michael Poryes and Steve Peterman, David Blocker

Produced by Alfred Gough and Miles Millar

Directed by Peter Chelsom

Walt Disney Pictures

Disney PRESS

New York

All rights reserved. Published by Disney Press, an imprint of
Disney Book Group. No part of this book may be reproduced
or transmitted in any form or by any means, electronic or
mechanical, including photocopying, recording, or by any
information storage and retrieval system, without written
permission from the publisher. For information address
Disney Press, 114 Fifth Avenue,
New York, New York 10011-5690.

Printed in the United States of America

First Edition
1 3 5 7 9 10 8 6 4 2

Library of Congress Control Number on file.
ISBN 978-1-4231-1816-9

For more Disney Press fun, visit www.disneybooks.com
Visit DisneyChannel.com

Chapter One

Even from the parking lot, everyone could hear the chant coming from inside the stadium: "Hannah! Hannah! Hannah! Hannah!" Outside, thousands of Hannah Montana fans spilled out of buses and cars and streamed toward the entrance. This was it! A Hannah Montana concert was about to begin!

As the audience entered the stadium, Mr. Stewart, Hannah's manager and dad, stood in her dressing room. He stared at the long, blond hair of the pop star and frowned. Something was wrong. Very wrong . . .

Hannah's *wig* was in the dressing room — but not Hannah!

Meanwhile, the crowd outside was getting even more frantic. The concert was sold out, but the screaming girls who didn't have tickets wouldn't give up.

Little did they know that even if they did get tickets, they might not see Hannah perform that night. That was because two of the girls trying desperately to get inside were Miley Stewart and her best friend, Lilly Truscott.

Miley Stewart was, of course, an ordinary high school student — but she had a very extraordinary secret: she was also Hannah Montana!

Not that that meant anything right now.

"The name is Miley Stewart," she told the ticket taker in desperation. *"Please.* We've got to get in there!"

"Our names are on the list!" Lilly added.

"Well, why didn't you say so?" the ticket taker asked. Then she rolled her eyes. "In your dreams, sweetcheeks. Next!"

Before Miley and Lilly could argue further, the people in line behind them pushed the girls out of their way.

Lilly shook her head. "You're the only pop star I know who can't get into her own concert," she told Miley.

Usually, being both Miley and Hannah served Miley well. She could be a world-famous pop star, and also have a normal teen life and normal teen friends. But lately having such a big secret had become harder and harder for her.

Suddenly, a security guard pulled up in

a golf cart and hustled over to do crowd control. Miley narrowed her eyes as she studied the cart. She had an idea. . . .

A few moments later, Miley and Lilly were driving down a backstage corridor toward Hannah's dressing room.

"Somebody stop those girls!" yelled the guard as he chased them.

"Can't you go any faster?" Lilly asked Miley.

"It's a golf cart!" Miley snapped back.

Finally, she saw it—Hannah's dressing-room door! Miley smiled with relief, especially when she saw her dad standing there. She screeched to a halt and made a dash toward him, with Lilly following.

Mr. Stewart held up his hand as the guard ran up, panting. "Whoa," he said. "It's okay. They're with me." Then he hustled the girls inside, where he turned to them and frowned.

4

"Sorry," Miley said. "Practice ran late and Jackson's car wouldn't start and—"

"Less explaining," her father interrupted, "more changing. We don't have a lot of time."

Miley knew the drill like the back of her hand. She went to the big wooden makeup box with the words HANNAH MONTANA painted on it and opened it up. Inside were rows of lipsticks and glittery eye shadows in every imaginable color. She pinned up her hair and tossed her old sneakers and sweatshirt aside, then sat down in front of the mirror.

Once her makeup was done, she pulled a short, sparkly dress over her head and zipped up her gold, high-heeled boots.

Finally, the long, blond Hannah wig was lifted off its special stand and placed on her head.

Miley turned to face the mirror. She smiled at her reflection.

Miley Stewart, ordinary high school girl, had vanished.

In her place sat Hannah Montana, international pop star. And she looked awesome!

Moments later, Miley was standing with her father. Slowly, the ceiling above them opened up, revealing the stage.

Miley smiled. "Love you, Daddy!" she hollered above the roar of the crowd.

"Lovin' you right back, darlin'," her father said.

The machinery began to lift Miley toward her cheering fans.

"Don't forget it's your turn to do the dishes tonight!" Mr. Stewart called.

"Oh, come on," Miley protested, "I did them last night."

Her dad grinned. "You're the one who wanted the best of both worlds. Watch your head!"

"Ladies and gentlemen," the announcer shouted. "Hannah Montana!"

Hannah stepped onto the stage to a blast of fireworks and the pulsing beat of her hit song, "The Best of Both Worlds." The crowd went wild, and Hannah gave them everything they had hoped for—and more. It definitely wasn't easy being two people at one time, thought Miley as she sang and danced her heart out. But at times like this, it sure was worth it!

Chapter Two

The next day, Hannah was still singing "The Best of Both Worlds." But this time she was in the middle of a beach party doing dance moves in the sand. When she got to the end of the song, she smiled and held the last note. . . .

"Cut!" called the director of Hannah's latest music video. "Hannah, as always, fabulous. That's a wrap, people. Good work."

Miley headed to the large tent that had been set up as her dressing room. Then, once inside, she eagerly sat down at her dressing table and started to take off her wig.

Fortunately, she glanced in the mirror first. A goofy-looking guy was peeking out from behind her clothes rack!

Miley screamed.

"No. It's okay. I'm sorry," the guy stammered. "I just had to meet you. I promised my girls that I'd say 'hi' to you for them." He took a deep breath. "Hi."

Miley took a long look at the intruder. He had thick glasses and buckteeth. His voice sounded friendly, even a little folksy. And he was wearing a T-shirt with a photo of his daughters on the front. All in all, he seemed harmless enough.

On the other hand, he *had* been hiding in her tent. . . .

As if he sensed her doubts, the man pulled out a crumpled piece of paper. It was covered with notes written in bright pink ink.

"My girls even wrote out some questions, if you have a second. Omigosh, this is such a thrill." He pulled out a camera. "Do you mind?"

Miley relaxed. This guy was a little offbeat, but he sounded sincere. "No," she said. "Go ahead."

Then a sharp voice suddenly cried out, "Don't even think about it!"

Vita, Hannah's publicist, burst into the tent.

"Vita, it's okay," Miley said.

"Nothing about this man is okay," Vita snapped. "Hello, *Oswald*."

The man took off his glasses. "Hello, Vita," he said, now in a British accent. "Looking lovely as ever."

Oswald took out his fake buckteeth and

10

Miley stared at him, astonished. Without his fake teeth and glasses, he looked like a completely different person.

"Oswald Granger," Vita said to Miley. "Chief sleaze for *Bon Chic*, England's most notorious tabloid."

"And we would love, with a capital O-V-E to do a cover feature on the global phenomenon that is Hannah Montana," Oswald added.

"And by 'feature,' he means career-ending exposé," Vita told Miley. She turned to Oswald. "'Country girl living her dream — beloved by millions.' That's all we got. That's all you're getting. Now get out."

Oswald shrugged. "You can't blame a bloke for trying." Then he walked out, leaving Miley somewhat shaken and wide-eyed.

"How you could even think we'd have

something to hide—" Vita called after him. Then, as soon as he was gone, she turned to Miley. "He didn't see anything, did he?" she asked.

Miley shook her head. "I don't think so."

"Good." The publicist sighed. "Don't talk to *anybody* unless I'm by your side," she reminded Miley. "I'm your publicist. I can't protect you if you don't let me. That's why you hired me, remember?"

Miley raised an eyebrow. "I didn't hire you. Remember? My record company did."

"Because they love you very much and want to be sure that you're treated like the superstar that you are," Vita replied smoothly. She caught sight of a notebook lying open on the table. "What's this?" she asked.

"Nothing," Miley said quickly. "Just a song I'm writing."

"On your own?" Vita asked, surprised.

"That is so sweet, but you have people for that. Hannah, honey, you need to concentrate on what you do best—singing your scrappy, blond heart out. Let me worry about everything else." She gave Miley a meaningful look. "Like making sure your little secret *stays* a secret."

The publicist sat down as Miley pulled off her Hannah wig.

"Sometimes I wish I could just stay Hannah," Miley said as much to herself as to Vita.

"You and me both, kid," Vita said. She nodded toward the tent opening. "Anyway, I'm never going to be able to get you out of here as Miley. Put Hannah back up and let's take you home."

Miley nodded and plopped the blond wig on her head. Then Vita grabbed the Hannah box and opened the flap of the tent. A swarm of reporters was waiting for them outside.

"Outta the way, you jackals!" Vita shouted. "Coming through. That's right, move aside. Please don't touch the pop star."

Miley followed, flashing her Hannah smile at the paparazzi.

Neither Vita nor Miley noticed Oswald dart back into the tent to retrieve his camera. They'd never noticed it on the chair, close to Hannah's dressing table . . . or its red RECORD button blinking. Luckily, Vita unknowingly kept turning it on and off as she sat in front of it so the reporter couldn't hear everything.

Oswald watched the recording later, his eyes wide with glee. If only Vita hadn't been sitting in front of the lens the whole time! He couldn't see much, but he could hear Vita talking about Hannah Montana's "little secret." But what *was* it? He had to know.

He quickly called his editor to give her the scoop.

"Talk to me, Ozzie," she said, "and don't disappoint."

"Apparently, there's a *secret*," Oswald reported.

"Find me that secret!" Lucinda, the editor, told him. "Hannah Montana is the most popular teenager in the world."

Oswald rolled his eyes. "Tell me about it," he said. "When my girls heard who I was coming to interview, Daddy suddenly had a real job, ha-ha-ha. . . ."

He quickly realized that Lucinda wasn't laughing.

"Mess this up," she snapped, "and Daddy won't have any job at all!"

Chapter Three

The next week it was back to real life for Miley—time to focus on stuff like her best friend Lilly's Sweet Sixteen party. Finally! It seemed as if they'd been planning it forever.

"As soon as the bell rings, we've got to bolt," Lilly told their friend, Rico, in gym class at Seaview High School. "There are like a million things left to do for my party."

"Lilly, reeeeeeeelax," Rico said as they waited to be picked for volleyball teams. "You hired Rico to cater your Sweet Sixteen, and Rico always delivers." Just then, Rico's name was called and he jumped up to join his team.

"*You're* bolting, right?" Lilly said to Miley.

Miley nodded. Then she remembered her brother, Jackson, was leaving that afternoon to go to college. "I just have to meet my dad and Jackson after school for one final, 'so leave already,' then I'm totally there."

"I just wish you'd been around more to help me plan everything," Lilly told her.

"I'm sorry," Miley said. "I had the tour. But now I'm here for good. Why are you so nervous? It's going to be an amazing party."

But plans changed after class when Vita came looking for Miley at school.

"Fabulous news," Vita told her. "Beyoncé has double pneumonia and has to drop out of the New York Music Awards. You're in!"

"*Aaah!* That's great!" Miley squealed with delight, then put on a more sober expression. "Not about Beyoncé. I should call. . . . But that's huge! What am I going to sing? What am I going to wear?"

"Great minds," said Vita, grinning. "I have the car and the Hannah box waiting for you. Hannah has got to do a major shop. Right now. Last chance."

Miley happily followed Vita, then suddenly stopped at the sound of her name.

"Miley?" Lilly called from the school doorway. Where was she going? Lilly wondered. What about her party?

"Minor Hannah emergency," Miley yelled back with a quick wave. "But I'll be there. Promise."

* * *

Later that day, Mr. Stewart and Jackson sat in a car outside the high school, waiting for Miley to appear. Jackson was decked out in a bright orange University of Tennessee hat and T-shirt, along with a smug smile.

His father, on the other hand, looked worried. He glanced at his watch. "If she doesn't hurry up, you're gonna miss your plane. Where is that girl?" he muttered.

Had he known where his daughter was at that moment, Mr. Stewart wouldn't have been worried. He would have been furious. Because Miley, dressed as Hannah, was having a blast shopping with Vita on ritzy Rodeo Drive.

As they left yet another boutique, Miley paused to scribble a quick autograph for a fan, then she followed Vita down the street, her arms full of shopping bags.

"Now wasn't that fun?" Vita asked brightly.

Miley nodded, but she looked troubled. "It feels kind of weird having them give me all this stuff for free."

"Please." Vita waved a hand dismissively. "Do you know what a well-placed photo of you shopping is worth? You're a star. An icon. You wear it, touch it, look at it—and the world has to have it."

Vita and Miley were both so intent on their conversation that they didn't notice Oswald Granger following them, ducking in and out of doorways to avoid being seen.

"They owe it to you, Hannah," Vita went on. "Name it, and it's yours." She led Miley past a uniformed doorman and into a fancy department store.

"Hannah! Hannah Montana!" called

the manager. "It is so good to see you!"

Miley glanced at Vita. Who *was* this guy?

"What can I get you?" he asked eagerly.

"Nothing," Miley told him. "I'm fine. We're actually—"

"Water—sparkling, flat, tap—chips, dip, nachos, caviar, ice cream, cookie dough, cashews," he offered.

Suddenly, he didn't seem so weird to Miley. "You know, if you combined those last two things . . ." she said, brightening. "I didn't have a very big lunch."

"Done," the manager told her. "Please consider us your personal closet. Help yourself to anything you like."

Miley glanced around the floor. Everywhere she looked, smiling salesclerks were holding out gorgeous clothes, shoes, and jewelry for her inspection.

"Anything?" Miley asked.

"Anything," he said firmly.

She hesitated. "Well, I still need to get Lilly a present, so maybe . . ."

Soon Hannah was sitting down, surrounded by clothes. A clerk held up two pairs of shoes for her to consider.

"I don't know," Miley said, overwhelmed. "I can't decide."

"Decide?" echoed the manager. "Oh, no. No deciding. Too stressful. Take them both. We'll just add them to the pile."

He motioned to another clerk, who hurried over and held out her arms. There were six watches on each one.

"A watch," said Miley. "I totally need a new—" Then she noticed the watch faces. "Is that the time?! We've got to go!"

She suddenly jumped up and flipped open her cell phone. "I can't believe I— Eleven messages! Jackson! Lilly's present!

Lilly"—just then, her frantic gaze zeroed in on a pair of gorgeous shoes—"will love *those*!"

She grabbed a shoe just as another hand reached over and grabbed its mate. Irritated, Miley glanced up, only to see that the other hand belonged to supermodel Tyra Banks!

"Sorry, I saw them first," Tyra said coolly. She turned to the manager. "Wrap them up, please."

The manager glanced frantically from the supermodel to the pop star.

"They're for my best friend," Miley said, pleading.

"How funny," Tyra replied. "They're for *my* best friend, too."

"My best friend's a size six," Miley said.

Tyra lifted one eyebrow. "How funny. *My* best friend's a size six."

The manager felt his heart racing. "Um, that's our only pair," he said.

Tyra glared at him. "That's not funny," she snapped. "Don't you know who I am?"

Two can play at that game, Miley thought. She smiled sweetly at the manager. "Well, I know you know who *I* am," she said.

The manager's head was spinning, and he thought he might faint. In fact, he kind of hoped he *would* faint when Tyra and Hannah actually began fighting over the shoes. Displays fell and customers ran out of the store screaming.

From behind a column, Oswald stepped out holding a camera. "Hello, front page!" he said, beaming, as he captured the brawl.

Chapter Four

A short time later, Hannah finally left the store, bruised but laden with a car full of clothes. Miley didn't know what she was going to tell her dad when she saw him. And Vita, who as a publicist should have been able to come up with a good story, was being no help at all.

"'Relax'?!" Miley said for what felt like the hundredth time. "Have you met my dad? He is not going to just 'shake off' me forgetting to say good-bye to Jackson." She frowned at the cars in front of them. "Come on, people, we need to move!"

As their limo pulled away from the curb, Oswald, still unnoticed, made a U-turn in his own car and slipped in behind them.

Inside the limo, Miley gazed at her loot. "And I didn't even get the shoes," she said sadly. "I'm the worst friend in the world."

She opened her Hannah box and started to take off her wig. Suddenly she spotted Oswald's reflection in the box's mirror.

"It's him!" Miley shouted.

Instantly, Vita banged on the divider between the driver and the backseat. "Step on it!" she yelled. "Let's lose this parasite."

As the limo sped up the Pacific Coast Highway, Oswald stepped on his accelerator. Now that he was hot on the trail of Hannah

Montana, there was no way he was going to let her escape!

The limo raced past the pier, where, Miley could see, Lilly's party was already in full swing. Miley watched it flash by, then turned to Vita in a panic. She couldn't let Oswald see Miley get out of the limo; he'd be sure to guess the truth. But she *had* to go to Lilly's party. . . .

"I can't get out of the car looking like Miley, and I can't show up at Lilly's looking like Hannah!" she cried.

Just then, her cell phone rang.

Miley looked at the caller. It was Lilly. She took a deep breath and answered. "Hey, Lilly," she said. "What's up?"

"Miley, we've talked about this party since we were, like, eight," Lilly said, clearly hurt. "Where *are* you?!"

"Don't worry, we're almost there," Miley

said, as the limo drove past the party again. "Well, we were . . ."

She listened for a moment. "Lilly?" She turned to Vita. "She hung—"

But before she could finish her sentence, the phone rang again. It was her father.

"Miley!" he said when she answered. "Lilly's mom wants to cut the cake and you're—"

"There is nobody in this household by those names!" she cried, then quickly hung up. She turned to Vita. "This is not good."

Vita rolled her eyes. "Puh-lease. Do you know how much you could charge for personal appearances?"

Personal appearances?! thought Miley. This is my best friend's birthday party! Which I'm missing! I'm a terrible friend.

Lilly's party was still in full swing. Dozens

of people were eating, dancing, and taking turns on the skateboard ramp Lilly had set up on the pier.

Lilly took her own turn, zooming down and then up the ramp, flipping her board, and sticking a landing on the rim beside the cutest boy in school. Lilly stared into his eyes as everyone around her cheered.

Then suddenly the boy pointed. "Is that Hannah Montana?!" he asked.

Lilly's eyes grew wide, and she lost her balance on her skateboard. She rolled back down the ramp and wiped out.

The next thing Lilly knew, Hannah Montana was running through the crowd to try to help her up. Still, as she held her hand, Lilly couldn't keep from glaring.

"I didn't have a choice," Miley tried to explain. "I swear I'll make it up to you."

Lilly didn't know how to answer, but

even if she had, there was no way that she could have. Her guests were so eager to get as close to Hannah Montana as possible that they pushed Lilly out of the way.

Things were out of control. Miley really needed help. But all she saw was Vita chasing Oswald down the pier in one direction, and her angry father marching toward her from the other. Still, maybe she could salvage the situation herself. . . .

"Uh, hey, everybody!" she called out. "I'm just here to wish my number one fan happy birthday. But don't mind me, because the whole day is about Lilly!" She pointed in Lilly's direction, but no one turned around. "Who's right over there, behind you," Miley went on, trying to push through the crowd. "Look." She managed to get to Lilly, but the fans were still totally focused on Hannah.

"You will never, ever, *ever* be able to make this up to me," Lilly fumed.

Miley's smile slipped. This was bad. This was *worse* than bad.

Meanwhile, all around them, the crowd began chanting, "Sing!"

Miley had thought things were out of control before. Now it seemed as if a riot was about to break out!

"Hadn't really planned on sing—" she began weakly.

She didn't want to steal the spotlight, really she didn't. But suddenly she was being lifted onto the stage and someone was handing her a microphone and everyone was cheering. . . .

And if there was one thing Hannah knew how to do, it was to take control on the stage.

She said a few words to the band members,

who were set up for Lilly's party, then turned back to the crowd. "This is for Lilly," she called out. "Five, six, seven, eight—"

She began belting out a song, and everyone immediately started jumping along. At the end of the chorus, she caught Lilly's eye.

"Sorry," she mouthed.

But Lilly just turned and walked away.

"You!" a voice with a funny accent called to her. "Wait. Birthday girl. I have some questions."

Lilly turned to see Oswald hurrying up behind her.

"Is it true that Hannah's really forty-three years old?" he asked eagerly.

Lilly rolled her eyes. She just wanted to be left alone.

"That she lip-synchs?" he went on.

Lilly frowned and kept on walking.

"That she grew up in a notable neighbor-hood in Nashville?" he persisted.

At last, she'd had enough. "More like a cornfield in some place called Crowley Corners," Lilly muttered, still furious at her "friend."

"Really?" Oswald's voice betrayed his interest. "How do you spell 'Crowley'?"

Lilly hesitated. She hadn't meant to tell this pushy reporter anything about Hannah—despite the fact that she'd ruined her party. After all, Lilly *had* been sworn to secrecy . . .

Then Lilly glanced back at the stage, where Hannah was now dancing with *her* cute guy. She felt her heart harden as she turned to Oswald. "Just like it sounds," Lilly said.

Chapter Five

The next morning, Miley stood on the beach behind her house, speed-dialing Lilly over and over again. "Why won't you answer?" she muttered.

Vita, meanwhile, was sitting on the Stewarts' deck, working on her laptop, when a newspaper landed with a plop on the keyboard.

"Have you seen this?!" Mr. Stewart asked.

A huge picture of Hannah and Tyra Banks wrestling over shoes was splashed across the front page.

"Oh, I know," Vita said brightly. "It's everywhere. It's fabu—" Then she suddenly noticed Mr. Stewart's frown. "Horrible," she said instead. "Bad Hannah."

"She and I need to have a little conversation," Mr. Stewart said, and he angrily marched across the sand toward Miley.

"Now?" Vita asked as she trailed behind him. "She's supposed to be getting ready to go to New York."

Mr. Stewart turned just long enough to give her a scorching look.

"Didn't she tell you?" the publicist went on. "It's really an amazing oppor—"

"I know about New York," he said curtly. "I got cc'ed in an e-mail."

Vita's face cleared. As long as Miley's

dad knew about the music awards, she thought, everything would be fine. . . .

But she was wrong.

"Not happening," he said flatly. "We're flying to Tennessee for Grandma Ruby's birthday." He smiled at Vita's astonished reaction. "Didn't she tell you?"

Next he turned to Miley, who was still redialing her phone.

"A shoe fight?" Mr. Stewart said in disbelief. "You got into a *shoe fight*?!"

"In my defense," Miley said, finally closing her phone, "I totally saw those shoes first."

Her father shook his head. "This is completely, totally, absolutely unacceptable. Actually, that pretty much describes all of your behavior lately. Standing up your brother, humiliating Lilly at her own party."

Vita rolled her eyes and pointed at her watch. Fatherly lectures were all well and good, but they had a plane to catch! Miley took the hint and started back to the house.

"I know I screwed up," she said to her dad. "I'm sorry. But I can't talk about this now. I have to go to New York. It's the music awards."

"So your grandma's birthday doesn't even —" her father began.

"Daaaad," Miley interrupted. "This is different and you know it."

"Yeah, in the grand scheme of life, *one* of these things is actually important," he said.

"Look, Robby," Vita broke in. "Mr. Ray. Father Montana. I know you think this calls for some kind of homespun 'talking to,' but Hannah's not going really isn't an option."

Mr. Stewart gave her an icy stare. "Her name's Miley."

"And *Miley* will be back before she leaves," Vita said brightly. "She's a superstar—we'll get her a private jet if we have to."

"Yes!" Miley's face lit up with excitement. "I always wanted one of those!"

Her father took a deep breath and counted to ten. "Fine. You win," he said, looking at Vita. "But you heard our superstar. She wants a jet."

"Really?" Miley couldn't believe it.

"I like your thinking," Vita said. "It'll take a little while to arrange, but I'll go on ahead to New York and set up the meet-and-greet." She whispered to Miley, "He's not nearly as bad as you said."

Miley nodded, though she couldn't help but be suspicious. Her dad had a little smile on his face that she didn't like one bit. . . .

Still smiling, Mr. Stewart lowered his window shade as he relaxed in the private jet. The bathroom door banged open and

Miley, dressed as Hannah, struggled to get out with her Hannah box intact.

"Next time you might want to demand a jet with a bigger bathroom," she said.

"Why are you getting all Hannah'd up?" her father asked.

She gave him a disbelieving look. "The Hannah-steps-off-the-plane photo op," she told him. "Balloons. Limo. Screaming fans. Like Vita says, it's all about the publicity."

He grinned and shook his head. "That Vita's just full of good advice," he said.

When the jet finally landed, Miley appeared in the doorway, striking a photo-friendly pose.

"Hello, New York!" she yelled.

Then her jaw dropped. They weren't in New York! They were in a field! Some-where in the country! With some cows and . . . Jackson?

"Looks like your limo's here!" Mr. Stewart said.

"**Y**ou can't do this!"

Miley was scrunched into the front seat of an old pickup with her dad, her brother, and a huge hound dog. "Okay, yes, maybe I should have remembered grandma's birthday."

"*I* did," Jackson said smugly.

"Not now, Jackson," Miley snapped. "Dad, Hannah Montana is supposed to be walking down a red carpet in New York in less than three hours."

Mr. Stewart's smile, which had been on his face for the last twenty-four hours, disappeared. "Miley, all your life all you've ever wanted was to sing," he said. "Hannah let you do that and still have a normal life. That was the dream, remember? That's why we created her in the first place. But I don't know if that's what she's about anymore."

"What are you saying?" Miley asked, even though she had a bad feeling that she didn't want to hear the answer.

"I'm saying I think we might be done," he said simply.

Miley's eyes widened with shock. "You can't take Hannah away from me!"

"Really?" her dad said. "'Cause that's what I'm doin'."

"No!" she cried. "Stop the truck! I'm not going to do it. I want to go home."

Mr. Stewart pulled the truck over and Miley got out, slamming the door behind her. Her dad followed her.

"You are home," he said. "Look around."

But Miley shook her head. "Hannah means everything to me," she said.

"And that right there might just be our problem," he answered.

Miley stared at her dad, then finally said, "I can never be Hannah again?"

"Ask me in two weeks," Mr. Stewart told her. "Let's see if the country girl still exists."

"Two weeks?!" she said.

He grinned. "Think of it as a Hannah detox. Now take off that wig and get in the truck."

"No!" she said suddenly, stomping her foot. She wasn't giving Hannah up so easily. "I am not getting in that truck. And I am most definitely not—"

Miley stopped as she felt her wig being lifted off her head. She raised her hand and turned around to see a tall, gray mare with a mouthful of blond hair.

"Aaah!" Miley cried, grabbing the other end of the wig. "Give that back, you mangy—"

Mr. Stewart shook his head. "Girl doesn't even recognize her own horse," he said. "Now that truly is sad."

He grinned as the horse let go of the wig, and Miley fell back on the road. She looked up at the horse. "Blue Jeans?" she said.

"Why don't we meet you at the house?" Mr. Stewart said as he climbed back into the truck. "It's just about a mile up the road. Don't forget your suitcase!" he shouted as he drove away.

Chapter Six

Miley stared down the dirt road, which seemed to go on forever, and decided that riding her horse was the only way to go. She dragged her Hannah box next to Blue Jeans and tried her best to pull herself and her suitcase up and onto the horse's back.

"Blue Jeans, you've got to hold still," she said. "Blue Jeans, please, don't move until—*Oof*!"

The next thing Miley knew, she was back on the ground, and Blue Jeans was loping across the pasture.

"Blue Jeans!" she called out in despair. "Blue Jeans, come back! *Please*." Her shoulders slumped. "Now what am I supposed to—"

"*Yah!*"

She turned at the sound of a loud voice behind her. It was a boy on his own horse. Within seconds, he'd galloped past Miley and lassoed Blue Jeans. He trotted back to Miley, as she hurried to hide her chewed-up Hannah wig.

"You okay?" the boy asked.

Miley squinted up at him.

"Blue Jeans doesn't really take to strangers," he went on. "Even dirty, sparkly ones."

Miley finally found her voice. "I know. She's *my* horse."

The boy looked at her more closely. "*Miley?*" he said.

She gave him a blank look in return.

"It's me. Travis," he said. "Travis Brody? We were in first grade together. Don't you remember? The last time I saw you was when we went swimming at your Uncle Earl's farm and both of us got poison oak all over our—"

Miley quickly held up her hand. "I remember you. Okay." It was not the most pleasant of memories. "I also remember you hanging me headfirst down a well."

Travis grinned. "Yeah. I guess I had a pretty big crush on you back then. But don't worry, I'm over it."

She smiled back at him. Hmm, she thought. Good to know.

The two of them decided it would be

easier for Miley to ride with Travis and lead Blue Jeans on a rope.

"Don't come around here too often any more, do ya?" Travis said as they trotted along.

"Often enough," said Miley, shrugging.

"How long you staying?" he asked.

"Two weeks," she said glumly as wistful images of New York City drifted through her head.

"Good luck with that." He chuckled.

Miley stiffened. "What's *that* supposed to mean?"

"Considering what you're wearin' and the fact you couldn't get on your horse, I'm guessing you've gone all California on us," he replied.

"I have *not*," she protested. "And you've only seen me for, like, two seconds. You don't know anything about me. Or California."

"Let me guess," Travis said, teasing. "Celebrities are regular folk, just like you and me."

"*Some* are," she replied. What did a country bumpkin like him know about celebrities anyway?

"Uh-huh." Travis sounded skeptical. "You actually know any?" he asked.

Did she know any? Sweet niblets! Miley couldn't resist. "I know Hannah Montana," she said.

"Really? Hannah Montana?"

Miley nodded. "I practically saved her life surfing the other day," she boasted. "She owes me big time. We're, like, *best* friends."

Travis raised his eyebrows, and Miley smiled. She could tell he was *very* impressed.

Just then, they reached the rambling country farmhouse where Miley's grandma Ruby lived. There was a large red barn in the distance, a big porch on the front of the house, and music and laughter spilling out from the open windows. No place could have seemed more welcoming. Still, Miley hesitated.

"I'm sure they're all waiting for you," Travis said. "I'll put Blue Jeans away."

"You don't have to do that," she told him.

He shrugged. "Kind of my job. I'm helping your grandma out for the summer."

She dismounted, and he handed her suitcase down to her.

"This is usually about the time someone would say thank you," he said.

Miley blushed. "I was getting there," she told him.

"No need," he said easily as he turned his horse around. "See you around, Smiley Miley. Remember? That's what I used to call you."

He trotted off toward the barn, and

Miley half smiled as she watched him go. "I remember," she murmured.

Then she turned back toward the house and began to climb the steps. She was more nervous than she'd expected. Inside, old friends and family members were singing a classic country song. In the middle was Grandma Ruby, clapping along.

Miley took a deep breath as she stepped through the door. Her grandmother's face lit up as soon as she saw her.

"Miley!" she yelled, and everyone cheered the new arrival.

"Miley, take the next verse," her dad called from the sofa.

But Miley froze. It had been so long since she'd been back home *and* since she had sung as anyone other than Hannah.

Everyone waited, then looked at one another.

"Sorry," she said meekly.

She was relieved when Grandma Ruby held out her arms and spoke up. "Well, I can't believe I just blew out my candles and I've already got my birthday wish," she said. "Come here, sweet thing."

Miley smiled gratefully. "Happy birthday, Grandma."

Her grandmother hugged her, then led her over to the dining-room table, which was covered with already opened presents. She picked up a plate with Elvis's face painted on it.

"Thank you for this," she told Miley. "I just love it! There's only one king," she added, "and I've been saving him a place of honor."

Carefully, she placed the plate in a hutch along with several others, each bearing the portrait of a different country music star.

"How long have you been planning this?" she asked Miley. "Must have taken you forever to find it."

Miley glanced at her father. "Apparently, I've thought of nothing else for weeks," she said.

After her grandmother hugged her again, Miley's dad pulled her aside.

"Hurt your grandma's feelings and a chewed-up wig will be the *least* of your worries," he whispered. Then in his normal voice he said, "It's time for cake. I'll collect the supper plates—you pass around forks. It'll give you a chance to say 'hi' to a few folks."

Miley handed out the forks, still feeling a little out of place. But before she was done, Jackson grabbed her and pulled her away.

"You're killing me!" he hissed. "You can't stay here."

"You think?" Miley asked sarcastically. "I'm outta here in two days."

"Yes!" Jackson raised his arms in jubilation. "Saved!"

Grinning, he turned to head back to the party, but Miley narrowed her eyes suspiciously and yanked him back.

"Saved?" she asked. "From what?"

Jackson rolled his eyes. "Dad," he said. "What else? On my back," he went on. "Watching my every . . ."

"Watching whaaaooo . . ." Miley stopped as the pieces fell into place. "Wait a minute." She studied Jackson's face. Yes. He was wearing that big-trouble expression.

"You didn't get into college," Miley said.

Jackson shrugged. "Who knew all those hard-and-fast deadlines Dad was always yelling about were actually hard and fast?" her brother said.

53

"So what *are* you doing?" Miley asked.

Jackson actually looked relieved to be confessing. "Cousin Derrick's got me working at his petting zoo until I can turn in my application. You remember Cousin Derrick?"

Miley winced just as good-old Cousin Derrick stepped into the hall to join them. The weaselly look on his face nearly matched that of the long, furry thing perched on his shoulder.

"Hey," Miley said, backing away. "What's with the rat?"

"Ferret," Derrick corrected her. "Harlow." He turned to look his pet in the eye. "We can keep a secret, can't we, Harlow?"

Miley glanced over at her brother. *Poor Jackson*, she thought.

Chapter Seven

By the time Miley returned, Grandma Ruby's party was in full swing. Everyone was talking, laughing, and enjoying the cake. And for the first time in days, Mr. Stewart felt relaxed. Ah, he thought, it's good to be home. . . .

Then Grandma Ruby came over. "Do me a favor and introduce yourself to Lorelai over there," she said. "She's new and a little shy."

He turned to look at her out of the corner of his eye. "You're not up to your matchmaking again, are you?" he asked.

He glanced across the room to check out this "shy" Lorelai—only to see a pretty woman laughing and talking away.

"Me?" said Grandma Ruby. "Never."

"Well, I'd hate for anybody to feel left out," Mr. Stewart said with a grin.

He took a deep breath and crossed the room, collecting plate after dirty plate from guests as he passed by. By the time he reached Lorelai, he had a stack of them in his arms. "Got anything for me?" he asked her.

"I don't know," she said, eyeing the stack of dishes. "Sure you can handle it?"

Mr. Stewart grinned. "You'd be amazed at what I can handle." Then he shifted the plates to shake her hand . . . and nearly dropped them.

Quickly, he spun around and just barely kept the plates from falling. "Told you, you'd be amazed," he said, a trifle smug.

Then he tripped over the sleeping hound dog, and the plates fell to the ground with a thundering *CRASH*.

Meanwhile, in New York, a crowd of tired and disappointed paparazzi were packing up their cameras, while Vita paced back and forth, wailing into her phone.

"The plane's empty," she said angrily. "Either they jumped or—" She paused to listen. "Well, how should *I* know where she is?" she snapped. She listened again. "Okay, yes, technically that is my job, but—"

Still talking, she brushed past an airport employee. He had a mustache and a potbelly, and, if she had looked closely, she would have seen it was Oswald Granger in yet another disguise.

As Vita headed in one direction, Oswald ran off in the other to chase down the pilot of the private jet.

"Hey, flyboy, wait up!" Oswald called to him. "I need the flight manifest."

The pilot shrugged and handed the document over. Oswald's eyes gleamed as he read the words written on it: CROWLEY CORNERS. Hannah Montana's secret wasn't going to stay a secret for long!

Grandma Ruby's party had officially ended, but a few stragglers still remained on the porch.

Above them, Miley sat in front of a dresser in one of the bedrooms. She held a framed photo of her mother and herself that was taken when she was four years old.

Her grandmother silently watched her from the doorway before she spoke up. "I keep thinking that I should change the wallpaper in here," she said. "But your mom picked it out when she was about your age."

"I like it," Miley said softly.

"You used to like a lot of things about coming to see me," Grandma Ruby said.

Miley looked over at her. "Grandma . . ." she began.

Her grandmother waved a hand. "It's okay. I know it's not personal. I just miss my Miley."

"Why do people keep *saying* that?" Miley asked.

"Maybe you should be asking *yourself* that question," her grandmother replied.

Chapter Eight

Early the next morning, a rooster crowed to greet the dawn, and, groaning, Miley reached up and pulled her pillow down over her head. It was *way* too early for anyone to get up.

"Miiiiley!" her dad yelled through her door. "Rise and shine!"

Miley sat bolt upright, her mind suddenly wide awake. "He wants his little country girl back, and he's going to get her," she said aloud to herself. Whatever her dad had dreamed up . . . two could play that game. "Commence Operation Save Hannah Montana!" she said.

Downstairs in the kitchen, Grandma Ruby was pouring coffee as Miley, wearing overalls and her hair in braids, appeared in the doorway.

"Mornin'!" she said brightly, with an exaggerated twang. "Sleep well? I've been up for *hours*. Hey, how about I feed the chickens and grab us some eggs? Like I always say, nothing better than fresh eggs for breakfast."

Then she skipped out the door.

A few minutes later, Miley was standing in the empty chicken yard with a bucket full of grain. She had done her share of work on the farm, but she had to admit it had been a while. She was a little rusty.

"Here, chick, chick, chick," she called out. "Come on, you stupid chickens, don't make me come in there, 'cause I will."

Miley smiled as she turned—then froze at the sight of what seemed like hundreds of beady-eyed birds. Nervously, she began to back away.

"Stay, chick, chick, chick," she said.

But, of course, they did not stay. Miley was holding their breakfast, after all.

From the porch, Mr. Stewart and Grandma Ruby enjoyed the show.

"How long you think before she figures out to put down the bucket?" Miley's grandmother asked, laughing.

Mr. Stewart just shook his head. He was laughing harder than Grandma Ruby.

By the time Miley figured it out, breakfast was long over.

Something was wrong, Mr. Stewart realized.
Hannah's wig was in the dressing room—
but not Hannah!

"Lilly, reeeeeeelax," Rico said. "You hired Rico to
cater your Sweet Sixteen, and Rico always delivers."

"Is it true that Hannah's really forty-three . . . she lip-synchs . . . and grew up in a notable neighborhood in Nashville?" Oswald, the reporter, asked Lilly.

"Hello, New York!" Hannah shouted when the jet finally landed. Then she realized she was actually in Tennessee.

Miley couldn't believe that Jackson wasn't really going to college!

"You're the *foreman*?" Mr. Stewart asked Lorelai
in surprise.

Miley asked Travis where he was taking her.
"To show you what you're missin'," he said.

Miley laughed as she watched Travis jump
into the water from the rope swing.

"I think I'm gonna add a little hip-hop
to this hoedown," Miley said to the crowd.

"So the mayor wants to host a big bash this evening in your honor," Lorelai told Lilly, who was pretending to be Hannah.

Hannah jumped in the broom closet and closed the door. Two minutes later, out jumped Miley.

"You know you're only wearing one earring?"
Travis asked Miley.

"How's the song coming?" Mr. Stewart asked Miley as
he looked out across Grandma Ruby's farm.

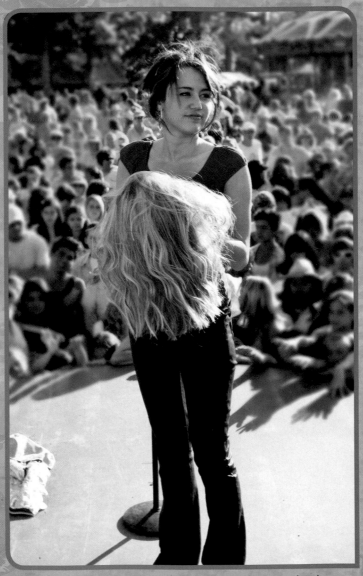

"The last time I stood on this stage, I was six. I was just Miley," she told everyone. Then she reached up and pulled off her wig. "I still am."

"Clean yourself up, honeybee," Grandma Ruby told her. "I'm taking you to the farmer's market. Robby Ray, my gutters need fixing and the truck's makin' sounds you just don't wanna hear."

He nodded. "I'm on it."

Grandma Ruby gave him a pleased smile. "If you need help, talk to the foreman. Should be by the vegetable patch. Just don't go squashing my squashes—they're prizewinners."

While Grandma Ruby took Miley to the farmer's market, Mr. Stewart went out to work on the pickup truck as he'd been told. When he got there, however, he found the foreman wearing a face mask and holding a welding torch.

Mr. Stewart banged on the fender to get the foreman's attention. "Looks like you beat me to it," he said.

Then the foreman stood up and took off the mask, and Mr. Stewart found himself face to face with . . . Lorelai.

"Lorelai," he said, surprised. "Ruby didn't . . . you're the *foreman*?"

"That would be me," she said.

He nodded toward the foreman's lodge. "So, uh, that means you're living here, too?"

"You're good at this," she said teasingly. "I was looking for a fresh start, and I guess Ruby thought the farm and I could both use some looking after, so . . ."

"She does like putting things together," Mr. Stewart said, nodding.

Meanwhile, Grandma Ruby and Miley bounced down the road with a truck full of watermelons. As Grandma Ruby drove, Miley scanned the radio for a station with halfway decent music. She suddenly realized it had been more than a day since she'd heard anything close to hip-hop or pop.

"You can keep trying," her grandmother told her, "but all you're going to find is country."

Miley sighed and stared out the window. She *so* couldn't wait to get her life back!

They came to a stop at a railroad crossing, and Miley noticed a large sign in the shape of a giant cow udder. The words SAVE CROWLEY MEADOWS were painted across it, along with FUND-RAISER THIS SATURDAY. The udder, which was painted to show how much money had been raised, was not very full.

"Uh, what's with the giant udder?" Miley asked. "*There's* something you'd never see in LA."

Her grandma shook her head sadly. "Old

Man Crowley died and left the town the Meadows," she explained. "Pretty much everything you can see. But we don't have enough money for the taxes, so I've been helping organize a fund-raiser or two. Oh, it's just awful . . ." she said.

The train passed, and the picture-perfect image of Crowley Corners came into view. It was no LA, but still . . . Miley had almost forgotten how lovely the little town was.

"Developers are circling like vultures," Grandma Ruby went on. "Talking about putting up apartment buildings, shopping malls."

"A mall?" Miley perked up. "Really?" To her that seemed exactly what a place like Crowley Corners needed.

"If they have their way, there won't be any open land left," her grandma said bitterly.

"Yeah," said Miley, "but at least you'd

finally have a decent place to—" She glimpsed her grandmother's face and decided, wisely, not to say more. "That's horrible," she said instead. "Who'd ever wanna change one lick of this place?"

"You'd be surprised," Grandma Ruby said. They had just reached the market, and she pointed to a slick-looking man handing out brochures. "I swear, every-thing about that man, Mr. Bradley, bothers me," Grandma Ruby told Miley. "You know, he only buys seedless watermelon? I mean, what's the point of eatin' watermelon if you can't spit the seeds?"

They set up their booth, and after a while Miley's grandmother gestured to a shoe store across the street. "When we're finished, maybe you and I can do a little shopping," she suggested.

"In there?" Miley rolled her eyes. The

shoes in the window looked at least a generation out of style. "No thanks, I'm good."

"Look, missy," Grandma Ruby snapped. There was a fire in her eyes. "You might be some fancy-pants back home, but here we're britches and boots, and if that ain't good enough for you, then maybe you should just pack up and get."

Miley stared back at her grandmother, not sure how to react to this stern talking-to.

"You might be fooling your daddy, but you sure as heck ain't fooling me," Grandma Ruby went on. Then her face grew softer, and she laid her arm gently around Miley's shoulders. "Now, I'm sorry for fussing at you, but I just think you should consider yourself lucky that for the time being you have a place like this to call home."

Miley nodded slowly. "I do." She knew what her grandma was saying. "I'm sorry."

"I know you are," said Grandma Ruby. "Now finish up here." She nodded toward Mr. Bradley. "I'm going to take this mood of mine and put it to good use."

While Miley cut a watermelon into pieces for sampling, Grandma Ruby gave the developer a piece of her mind.

"Have all the little fund-raisers you want," replied Mr. Bradley, as he stood by a model of his mall. "You won't be able to stop progress."

"Excuse me," Miley suddenly heard someone say behind her. "Do you know this girl?"

She glanced at the next booth, where a vendor was selling homemade sauces. The voice belonged to that reporter, Oswald

Granger! And he was holding a picture of Hannah Montana!

"Sure," the vendor said, insulted. "It's Hannah Montana. I don't live under a rock."

"No, obviously not, but I meant actually *know* her," Oswald persisted. "Or her family, perhaps?"

Her heart racing, Miley dropped to her knees, then peeked over the counter. That pestering paparazzo was one of the reasons she was stuck here in the country, instead of performing in New York!

"Really?" Oswald was saying. "Never? But my sources are impeccable." Oswald sighed and reached for a sample of the man's sauces. "May I try the . . . ?"

He crammed several crackers in his mouth.

"I wonder if she used a different name," Oswald went on with his mouth full. He was so focused on the mystery of Hannah Montana, in fact, that he didn't even notice Miley sneak up and switch the sauces. She traded the mild tomato sauce for a jar labeled DEVIL LEVEL HOT.

When the vendor turned his back, Oswald grabbed more crackers, smeared them with the hot sauce, and began stuffing them in his mouth. At the same time, Miley slipped away from the booth, over to a truck loaded with walnuts. Quietly, she unlatched the back, and soon a cascade of nuts was flowing down a slight hill between the stalls.

Meanwhile, Oswald's mouth was beginning to burn—badly! He looked around frantically and saw a dog bowl filled with water. He grabbed it and gulped, but even that didn't work. He spit out the water and ran around looking for something that could put out the fire . . . and that's when he stepped on the walnuts.

Oswald's feet flew out from under him and he fell backward, right onto Mr. Bradley's model of Crowley Meadows.

Mr. Bradley stared down at him, horrified.

"Terribly, terribly sorry," Oswald managed to gasp.

"You're forgiven," Grandma Ruby said sweetly, marvelling at the mess. "Miley, come over and help me with this poor man."

Reluctantly, Miley stepped up and helped Oswald to his feet.

"You're too kind. Really," he mumbled, his mouth still not fully recovered. Then he looked at Miley more closely. "Hey," he said, "you're about the same age. Do you know this Hannah Montana?"

"Hannah Montana?" Miley replied in

a sudden, exaggerated drawl. "Who don't know Hannah Montana? She's famous."

"Well, she's telling people she's from this little patch of nowhere—but no one's ever seen her," Oswald said.

"I've seen her," said Miley, still using a superthick Southern accent. "Saw her. Know her. Knew her."

"Then you're the only one," he said. He looked eager and excited.

"I know all the Montanas-es," Miley went on.

"Know where I could find them?" Oswald asked, hardly daring to hope.

"Sure," Grandma Ruby chimed in. She winked at Miley. It was time to put this hunting dog off the scent. "You go about five miles south of town, take a right at the first crick. . . ."

"Take a left at the second crook," Miley added.

"And there you are," said Grandma Ruby.

Oswald looked down at his map, slightly confused, and Miley and Ruby grinned as he shrugged and walked away.

Hours later, Oswald was still looking at his map as he stood in front of an old, abandoned cabin next to a muddy, weedy creek.

"Hello?" he yelled. "Anybody home?"

Suddenly, his phone rang.

"*What?*" he yelled, annoyed.

It was his boss, Lucinda. "A better question might be *where*?" she told Oswald. "As in *where's* my story?"

Just then, Oswald's phone beeped to tell him he had another call. "Two seconds, love," he said. "Hello?"

Oswald's daughters, Phoebe and Clarissa, were calling from their boarding school.

"Daddy," Phoebe said. "Where are you? You didn't call."

"Sorry, darlings," Oswald said. "Daddy's working. I'll call you back in two seconds."

"Hurry," said Clarissa. "It's almost lights out."

Oswald clicked back to Lucinda. "Sorry, Lucinda," he said. "Now don't worry, I guarantee this Hannah Montana story is . . ."

He was interrupted by his daughters' screams.

"Hannah Montana!" shouted Phoebe. "I don't believe it! Have you met her yet?"

"Tell us everything!" exclaimed Clarissa.

"Who's that?" snapped Lucinda. "What's all that screaming?"

"I'd thought I'd hung up," Oswald apologized. "Darlings, I'll call you back.

Promise," he told his girls. "Sorry," he told Lucinda. "You were saying?"

"Ozzie, I want the *dirt*," the editor said sharply.

"Trust me," he answered. "I'm all over it."

He closed his phone and groaned as he looked around the woods. Yeah, I'm all over it, he thought. As soon as I make it back to civilization, that is.

Chapter Nine

Later that day, Miley sat in Grandma Ruby's hayloft, strumming her guitar. She began to sing, but she knew the song needed work. Still, it was a start. . . .

Then, suddenly, Travis appeared, and Miley jumped.

"Sorry," he said, stepping back. "Don't stop. I'm goin'."

"It's okay," Miley told him. "I'm just goofing around."

"Hey, I think it's great you're still doing that singin' thing," Travis said.

Miley gave him a puzzled look. "Singing thing? What singing thing?"

"Come on, everybody knows that's all you ever wanted to do," he said. He reached for the toolbox he'd been looking for. "You actually got a nice voice."

Miley sniffed. "Thanks. I've heard that. So, uh . . . what did you think of the song? I wrote it."

"The song?" Travis asked.

"That thing I was just singing?" Miley said. She frowned a little. "Did I mention I wrote it?"

Travis grinned and nodded encouragingly. "And it sounded to me like you got most of the notes right, so . . . way to go, Miley."

He gave her a thumbs-up, then started back down the ladder.

"Most?!" she said. She got up and hurried after him. "So why didn't you like it?" she demanded as soon as she caught up.

"Geez, Miley," said Travis. "I didn't say I didn't like it."

"Well, you sure didn't say you did," Miley said.

He shrugged. "It wasn't bad," he said. "It just wasn't . . ."

"Good?" she offered.

". . . *about* anything," he said. "It didn't tell me who you are. What you feel."

She narrowed her eyes at him. "Know what I'm feeling now?" she asked.

"I've got an idea." He grinned. "Sorry. You asked."

He took out his hammer and began working on the old chicken coop, while Miley sank down to the ground to sulk. "Why are you even bothering with that?" she asked him.

"Starting up an egg business," he explained. "Me and Ruby struck a deal. I rebuild the coop, I get to sell the eggs."

Miley eyed the coop. It had definitely seen better days. "That's a lot of rebuilding."

"Hey, gotta start somewhere, right?" He pried a rotten board away from the frame. "Life's a climb . . ." he told her, smiling. "But the view's great."

"So that's really all you want to do?" Miley said. "Sell eggs in Crowley Corners?"

"Where else would I sell 'em?" Travis asked reasonably.

"That isn't what I meant," she said.

"I know what you meant." He nodded. "You just don't get this place at all, do you?" He looked at her for a moment, then set down his hammer. "Come on," he told her. "Let's go."

He walked over to the paddock and

began to untie their horses.

"Where are we going?" Miley asked.

He grabbed a cowboy hat off the fence and plopped it on her head. "To show you what you're missin'."

Minutes later, Miley was following Travis across the Tennessee countryside. They galloped through a field. Then they dismounted and tied up their horses and made their way through the woods until they reached a pond. Miley stared, delighted.

"This is our place!" she exclaimed. "I used to sneak out here all the time. I forgot it was even real. Look, there's jumpy rock. And the fort used to be over there. Remember? And our swing—" She grabbed an old piece of rope tied to a high branch. "It's still here. This is our swing!"

Grinning, Travis took the rope and

leaned out over the water. "So what do you think?" he asked. "Should we give it a try? Still looks —"

Before he could finish, the rope snapped, sending him splashing into the pond. He climbed out laughing, and a few minutes later he and Miley had tied on a new rope and were ready to swing.

It didn't take long, with Travis's help, for Miley to see what she'd been missing — and to be reminded that there was more to life than top-forty music and shopping malls. And Miley, in return, helped Travis with the chicken coop when they got back to the farm.

Miley also kept working on the words to her new song.

She still missed Hannah a little, but there was suddenly a lot more on her mind . . . including Travis.

Chapter Ten

Saturday soon came—the day of the town's big fund-raiser—and Miley actually found herself having a lot of fun. For one thing, she got to see her dad singing onstage, something he hadn't done often, she realized, since Hannah Montana had come along. Backing him up was a local band, which included Travis on the guitar.

As Mr. Stewart finished his song, the

audience whooped and hollered, and Travis grabbed the mic, yelling, "Robby Ray Stewart! Great to have you back, sir!"

Miley clapped for her dad and watched as Lorelai stepped up to give him a big, congratulatory hug. As soon as Mr. Stewart saw Miley, however, he awkwardly backed away. Lorelai looked hurt, and Miley was puzzled.

"What's the matter with him?" Miley asked her grandma Ruby. "He's dated before."

"Maybe it's starting to mean something again," Ruby suggested. Then she wrinkled her nose as Cousin Derrick and Jackson walked over. "Jackson, there's a smell comin' off you that'd make a skunk head for the hills," she declared.

"Must have gone a little heavy on the cologne," Jackson said. Then he leaned over close to Miley. "A raccoon vomited on my shoes. My job stinks. My life stinks. I stink," he groaned. He shook his head, then spied his dad approaching.

"I'm gonna jump on that key lime pie!" he announced, and quickly turned to go.

As Jackson hurried off, Mr. Stewart came over and sat down at Miley's table. She stared at him for a minute. "What?" he finally said.

"You like her," Miley said, nodding in Lorelai's direction. "She likes you. Why do you have to make everything so complicated?"

"Miley, you just don't under—" her dad began. Then he suddenly stopped. "How do you know she likes me?"

Miley rolled her eyes. "Because if she doesn't, there's something wrong with her."

Her dad half smiled. "You make a very good point," he said.

She playfully bumped him with her

shoulder. "Might want to help her out back. With the empties and all . . ."

Mr. Stewart blushed, then took her up on her suggestion.

He walked out back to where Lorelai was sorting bottles. "Sorry about that," he said, referring to their hug. "Back there. It's just . . . this trip's supposed to be about Miley, not about me."

"Ever think the two might be related?" Lorelai asked.

Mr. Stewart considered the idea for a moment. He hadn't thought of it that way. "You're right," he told her. "Sometimes I make things more complicated than they need to be. It's just our family is . . . closer than most, more . . ."

"Secretive?" Lorelai suggested. "I've noticed."

Mr. Stewart didn't know how to respond.

"Listen," she said, "it's cool. I mean it. If the time's right, you'll tell me." She gave him a warm smile, then added, "So how's Miley doing?"

Mr. Stewart glanced back into the hall to see Travis leading Miley onto the dance floor. "I have a feeling she . . ." He smiled at Lorelai. "*We* are going to be just fine."

Inside the hall, Miley and Travis danced to a slow song—and as far as Miley was concerned, it could have gone on all night long. But of course it didn't. Before Miley knew it, the song was over and Travis was stepping back to look her eagerly in the eye.

"Hey, Miley, come on. It's open mic," he said. "Wanna give it a try?"

"No, no, no. I'm good," she said. Sing in public? As Miley? That was too risky. "Thanks. My dad wouldn't . . ."

"It's just about having a good time is all it is," said Travis. Then he jumped up on the stage and grabbed the microphone.

"Looks like we got ourselves a taker!" he announced. "Right here! Come on up, Miley!"

Miley felt every eye in the place fall on her. She gulped and thought of her dad. . . . But what could she say? She slowly walked up and took the mic from Travis.

"Just let yourself go and have some fun. They'll come around," he told her.

It was almost funny, Miley thought, the way he was reassuring *her*—Hannah Montana! Almost. But then again, she was truly nervous. She hadn't sung as Miley in a very long time. But she didn't have much choice now.

"Hey, y'all," she said, waving shyly to the crowd. She took a deep breath, then went ahead and took the plunge. "If it's all right with you, I think I'm gonna add a little hip-hop to this hoedown," she told them.

She started clapping out a beat that the band began to copy, and pretty soon the audience was boogying along. Outside on the porch, Mr. Stewart and Lorelai were still talking. But it didn't take long for them to sense the energy from inside.

Mr. Stewart peered into the dance hall. *"Miley?!"* he said.

By the time he reached the dance floor, Miley had the whole crowd up and following her moves. They were having a great time — and so was Miley. Still, Mr. Stewart was a little anxious. This was hardly his idea of keeping a low profile. On the other hand, he did say he wanted his country girl back. And she was definitely back — big time.

Miley finished her number with one last

boot stomp, and the crowd went wild.

"Our own Miley Stewart, people!" Travis hollered.

Miley grinned, enjoying the cheers from everyone but Grandma Ruby, whose eyes were on the developer who'd just entered the room.

"You've got a lot of nerve coming in here!" she said, walking up to Mr. Bradley.

"I'm sorry, I thought this was a community event," Mr. Bradley replied.

"Community." Grandma Ruby practically spat out the word. "You don't even know what that word means."

"I know that your idea of it is a thing of the past," he answered. "How much did you raise tonight? A thousand dollars? Two thousand? Well, whatever it is, I'll double it."

A murmur ran through the crowd, but

Grandma Ruby snapped, "We don't want your money."

"Fine," he said, shrugging. "Because at the end of the day, it ain't gonna matter. You can have a hundred of these things—but you ain't never gonna raise the kind of money it's gonna take to buy the Meadows. Not unless The Beatles show up for a benefit concert." He pretended to think that over, then added sarcastically, "Oh, wait, small problem . . ." He chuckled.

Suddenly Travis turned to Miley. She knew what he was thinking—and she quickly turned away.

"So the sooner all of you just accept the inevitable," Mr. Bradley went on, "the sooner—"

"Miley knows Hannah Montana!" Travis suddenly shouted.

The room froze, and Miley turned back

to shoot him a "what do you think you're *doing*?" glare.

"Miley saved Hannah's life surfing," Travis went on obliviously. "They're best friends. She could help us. Maybe give a concert. That would raise a ton of money." He nodded to her, grinning. "Miley?" he said.

Every face in the crowd, it seemed, turned to her hopefully.

How could she ever say no? And how could she let Travis catch her in such a huge lie?

She smiled back at them meekly. "I guess I could give her a call. . . ."

Chapter Eleven

That night, Miley tried to take her mind off the mess she'd gotten into by working on her song. But she was still reeling. Her dad found her on the porch and took a seat beside her.

"Hey, caterpillar," he said. "How's the song coming?"

"Not great." She sighed. "I guess I'm still figuring out what I want to say."

"Just lead with your heart, honey," Mr. Stewart told her. "It'll come."

Miley bit her lip, then said, "I never should have told Travis about Hannah. I didn't mean for any of this to happen."

"I know you didn't," her dad said gently. He put his arm around her and gave her a comforting squeeze. "We'll deal with it. At least it's for a good cause."

"What about that reporter?" she asked, referring to Oswald. She knew he was still in town and would *never* leave when he heard Hannah Montana would be playing.

"What we really gotta worry about is how we're going to get Hannah here," Mr. Stewart replied.

Miley gave him a guilty smile.

Her father's eyes narrowed. "*Now* what have you done?"

* * *

The next morning, Mr. Stewart's question was answered when a long, black limo cruised through town. A dozen girls ran after it, autograph books in hand.

"Hannah!" they screamed. "Hannah Montana! Hannah!"

When the limo pulled up in front of Grandma Ruby's house, Miley bounded down the steps to meet it.

"She's here!" Miley shouted. "I didn't know if she'd really come!"

Then the limo door opened—and out stepped Lilly, wearing a Hannah Montana wig and big sunglasses. Miley raced over to hug her, and Lilly hugged her back, though not quite as eagerly as she would have before her party.

"Thank you! Thank you! Thank you!" Miley said.

Lilly shrugged. "Vita said I could keep the clothes," she replied.

Then Vita got out of the limo and looked around. "So rustic," she said. "I love it! Miley, this whole 'pop star saves town' angle is genius. Not so genius you're forgiven for ditching me in New York and almost costing me my job—but genius nevertheless."

Miley happily pulled Lilly's suitcase out of the trunk and led her up to the porch to meet Grandma Ruby. Then she hurried her inside.

Upstairs in her bedroom, Miley worked to repair the damage she'd done.

"I am *so* sorry," she said, taking Lilly's hands. "You're the best friend I ever had. When I thought you might not talk to me again . . . that I might lose you forever . . ."

"Hey, you couldn't lose me even if you

wanted to." Lilly grinned, then took off the Hannah wig and handed it to Miley.

"Good," said Miley, "'cause I never want to." Then the two friends hugged.

"Oh, and, um, sorry about talking to the reporter," Lilly said after a minute.

"What?" Miley let go of her. "*You're* the one who talked to the reporter?! Lilly, how could you?"

Lilly gave her a look. "I thought this was one of those 'you're sorry, I'm sorry' moments."

Miley took a deep breath and nodded. "It is," she said. "And I am." She hugged Lilly once more. "I swear, Hannah will never come between us again."

Suddenly, there was a loud knock on Miley's door.

"Miley?" Lorelai called.

"Yeah?" Miley said.

"Could I talk to you and Hannah for a minute?"

The girls froze in panic, then Miley quickly tossed the Hannah wig back to Lilly.

"Miley?" Lorelai called again from the hallway. "It's kind of important."

Finally, Miley opened the door.

"I'm sorry," Lorelai said as she spied "Hannah" lying on the bed. A wet towel lay over her head—covering Lilly's face. "I didn't realize—"

"It's okay," Miley whispered. "It's just one of those de-stressing things she has to go through. Helps with the jet lag."

"Jet lag?" Lorelai looked confused. "But California is only two hours—"

"Hannah only flies east to west," Miley said quickly. "So sometimes she has to take the long way around. She gains time." Miley grinned. "She's actually getting younger.

Did you want something?" she asked.

Lorelai tiptoed to the bed and leaned over Lilly. "Hannah?" she said softly. "I'm Lorelai. We're all just so grateful you're here."

"Whatever I can do to—" Lilly graciously began.

Then Miley suddenly grabbed her foot and twisted it—hard.

"Foot massage," Miley told Lorelai, grinning. "Pressure points. Relieves jet lag. Very LA."

Lorelai nodded as if this made sense, then turned back to Lilly. "I can't believe I have another favor to ask, but—"

"Ask away," Lilly said cheerfully. "There's a—"

She stopped as Miley gave her foot a sharp twist again.

"She's also not supposed to talk," Miley quickly explained.

Just then, Mr. Stewart called from below. "Miley. Are you up there?"

"He doesn't know," Miley said without thinking. Then, realizing Lorelai had heard, she added, "That Hannah's here. He'll be so excited. I've gotta tell him."

She looked down at Lilly. But how could she go?

As if reading her mind, Lorelai took Lilly's foot. "I'll take over," she said sweetly.

Miley's eyes cut to Lorelai, then back to Lilly. "Fine," she said. "But no talking!"

She ran down the stairs and to the front porch. "Dad?" she called. Then she spotted him climbing a ladder toward her window. "Dad! No! What are you doing?" she cried.

"Fixin' Grandma's gutters," he answered calmly. "Hold the ladder." He pointed to the vegetable garden behind him. "But don't squash the squashes."

As Miley ran over to help him, Lilly did her best silent-Hannah imitation upstairs.

Fortunately, Lorelai was doing enough talking for both of them. "So the mayor wants to host a big bash this evening in your honor," she said. "I'm having lobsters flown in from Maine, just for you. 'Course, there's no real point if you can't be there."

She kept rubbing Lilly's foot, then smiled as Lilly moaned. "Is that a yes?" Lorelai asked excitedly.

Lilly froze. She hadn't meant to make a sound—but Lorelai's foot massage had felt so good. There was no taking it back now, though. So she nodded and moaned again—just as Mr. Stewart reached the window and looked in.

He hurried back down the ladder. "What is Lorelai doing rubbing Hannah's feet?!" he asked Miley.

"Technically, they're Lilly's," Miley said.

"Stay!" Mr. Stewart ordered her as he marched into the house. He was going to get to the bottom of this—alone.

He burst into the bedroom and took Lorelai by the hand. "Come on now, why don't you just leave Hannah be and—"

"Shhh," Lorelai whispered. She pointed to the blond head. "I think she's asleep. But she said yes!" she went on, happily. "She's coming to the mayor's dinner. It was my job to get her there, and she said yes. You're goin', right?"

Suddenly, Mr. Stewart stopped thinking about Miley and Lilly and their latest scheme and focused on Lorelai. "I don't know," he said. "Is this you asking me?"

Lorelai smiled. "Yeah, I think it just might be."

"Well, then, this is me accepting."

Chapter Twelve

Later that day, as Miley and Lilly sat in the kitchen enjoying a batch of Grandma Ruby's cookies, Lilly glanced out the window to see Travis working near the fence.

"I want a cowboy," she said, sighing.

Miley followed her gaze and frowned. "That one's taken," she told her friend.

"Really?!" Lilly turned to Miley with a big smile.

"Yes." Miley nodded. Then she bit her lip. "No. Maybe. I don't know. . . . Looks like we're gonna be 'just friends.'" She shrugged, then brightened as an idea popped into her head. "But he hasn't met Hannah yet!"

She looked at Lilly and could see she had the same thought.

Maybe it was about time for Travis to meet Hannah Montana. . . .

A short while later, Lilly walked out of the house with Hannah Montana and headed straight for the fence where Travis was working.

Travis turned, clearly flustered to see Lilly and Hannah beside him.

"Oh, hi," he stammered. "I'm Travis. Thanks for comin'," he told Hannah.

"Happy to help," Miley said. She

grinned her biggest Hannah grin. "This is Lilly. She's my . . . assistant."

"*Executive* assistant," Lilly corrected her.

"Well, welcome to Crowley Corners," Travis said.

"Sure would be nice to have someone show us around," Lilly said warmly.

"Oh, real subtle," Miley muttered in her ear.

But Travis shuffled his feet. "I really don't think I'm your guy," he said awkwardly. "But nice meeting you." He smiled at them politely, then turned back to his work.

Miley's mouth dropped open. This wasn't how things usually went with Hannah Montana. She felt Lilly push her forward toward Travis, but she didn't know what to say.

"So. Putting up a satellite dish?" she finally blurted out.

"It's a birdbath," Travis said.

"I knew that," Miley said as Lilly snickered behind her. "Lilly, could you find the owner of this fine house and walk her through my dietary needs?" she said without turning around.

Lilly looked at her blankly.

"*Go*," Miley said, making a little shooing motion. "Assist."

Lilly slumped away, leaving Miley alone with Travis.

"So you and Miley are pretty close?" he asked after an awkward pause.

"You have no idea," Miley said.

"You don't have to answer if it's too personal, but . . ." Travis hesitated, then took the plunge. "Do you think she'd go out with me if I asked?"

Miley used every ounce of her self-control to sound casual. "You want to go out with Miley? Why haven't you asked her?"

"I just don't want to risk messing everything up if she doesn't like me that way," he explained.

"She *so* likes you that way," Miley eagerly said. Then she cocked her head. "Wait, you'd really rather be with *Miley* than show *Hannah Montana* around town?"

He ducked his head, grinning. "You'd be a real prize, don't get me wrong, but *Miley* . . . I can't help smiling when I'm around her. I think about her all the time."

"What are you telling *me* all this for?" Miley asked, laughing. "Go ask her out."

"Really?" said Travis. He started for the house. "Okay, I'll—"

"No! I mean, she's not *here*," Miley said quickly. She pretended to call for herself— "Miley?!" Then she shrugged. "See? Not here. I think she said something about grooming Blue Jeans in the barn. Yes. Barn." She pushed him in that direction. "Go look. Go. Go. Go."

Travis looked confused, but he did as he was told, and Miley sprinted back into the house, racing past Grandma Ruby and Lilly.

Travis searched the barn. But after finding no Miley, he soon returned.

Lilly met him on the porch. "Tried the kitchen?" she suggested.

Travis shrugged and went inside . . . just as Miley climbed out her window and down the trellis to the ground.

"Mess up my roses, and there's going to be heck to pay, young lady," Grandma Ruby warned.

Miley hit the ground and took off running, while Travis came back outside, looking even more bewildered.

"Tried the coop?" Grandma Ruby suggested.

With a sigh, Travis headed back in that direction. "Miley?" he called when he got there. "Miley, are you—"

"Hey, slacker!" she said, smiling and trying not to pant as she walked out from behind the coop with two paintbrushes in her hand. She handed him one.

"I was just talking to your friend Hannah . . ." Travis said slowly as they started to paint. "Actually, we were talking about you."

"Really?" Miley did her best to look surprised. "Was there something you wanted to ask me?" She caught herself. "I mean, say? Talk about?"

Travis kicked at the dirt. "I know you're going to have to go home soon and—"

"Yes!" Miley shouted. *Oops*, she thought,

kind of jumped the gun there. "Yes, that's right, Travis," she said more calmly. "Go on."

"I was wonderin' . . ." He was blushing. "I don't know if . . . Would you like to go to dinner with me tonight?"

Miley did not shout, turn a cartwheel, or jump for joy. Instead, she said, "Tonight? Um, sure. I don't think I have any plans."

Travis smiled, relieved. "Cool," he said.

Later that afternoon, Miley stood frozen in front of her mirror, holding up a dress, while her dad stood by the door.

"What do you mean, I can't go?!" she asked him.

"Hey, you're the one who promised Lorelai that Hannah would be the guest of honor at the mayor's big lobster hoo-ha tonight," he said.

"No, Lilly did," Miley protested. She

turned to her friend, who was seated on her bed.

"Actually, Hannah did," Lilly pointed out.

Miley shot her a look, then turned back to her dad. "But *I* promised Travis," she said.

"You know what?" he said. "I'll leave it up to you. I think you should do whatever you think is right." And with that he walked away.

Miley winced. She hated it when her dad left it up to her and her conscience!

She looked at her Hannah box, lying there open on her dresser, then back to her reflection in the mirror. Why did Hannah's dinner with the mayor and her own date with Travis have to be on the same night?!

Chapter Thirteen

At six o'clock sharp, Miley rode to the town hall in the back of Hannah's limo. There was no way she could miss the mayor's dinner, she'd decided. But who was to say that she couldn't have dinner with Travis, too?

Through the limo window, she saw Travis waiting for her in the fancy Italian restaurant across the street. He'll just have to wait a little longer, she thought, as she got out of the car.

A throng of fans surrounded her as she made her way into the hall. Once inside, she did the usual photo op with the mayor and his wife.

"Where's Miley?" Lorelai asked Mr. Stewart and Grandma Ruby, glancing at her watch. "She should be here."

"She's got East Coast West Nile disease," Grandma Ruby replied with a sorry nod.

Lorelai raised an eyebrow, but Mr. Stewart spoke up before she could ask anything else. "Whew," he said. "That thing's travelin' some. Must have skipped the fence at Tennessee."

As the guests took their seats, the mayor clinked his glass to make a speech.

"Be seated!" he said. He turned to Hannah. "And let me just say, honestly, to have someone with your talents, a true star, take an interest in our humble little corner of the world, well . . . Miss Montana, Hannah, if you will, what I'm trying to say is . . ." He paused. "What am I trying to say?"

"That we can't thank you enough," said Lorelai quickly.

"That's it!" The mayor beamed. "And if there's anything you need . . ." He turned to Hannah's suddenly empty seat. "Where did she go?"

Hannah was standing by the window, looking out across the square. She could see Travis still patiently waiting for her . . . or, that is, for Miley.

Miley sighed. Then she realized that every eye in the hall was on her. She replayed the mayor's last words in her mind. "Need?" she said. "Oh . . . I just need to check on my fans."

She opened the window a crack and let in the sound of her fans' screams. "See?" She grinned. "They need me. I need them. But you know what I really need?" she added. "To use the bathroom." She cut her eyes to Lilly and grabbed her hand. "Come with!"

As Miley pulled Lilly down the back stairwell, all she could think about was Travis. "He said so many nice things about me to Hannah." She sighed. "I can't wait to hear him say them to me."

"You do know you're actually the same person, right?" Lilly reminded her. Then she pointed to a broom closet. "Hannah box is in there. Quick."

Hannah jumped in and closed the door. Two minutes later, out jumped Miley.

"I'll be right back," she told Lilly. "Cover for me."

Then she raced out the revolving doors on the side of the town hall to avoid all the fans out front. No one saw her leave . . . except one young fan named Cindy Lou.

Moments later, Miley slid into the seat across the table from Travis. "Sorry I'm late," she said.

"You're not late. I was early." He grinned, then looked at her more closely. "You know you're only wearing one earring?"

Miley put her hand to one ear in surprise. "Trendy LA thing," she said as she slipped off the earring.

"Guess you're gonna be heading back there pretty soon, huh?" Travis said. He bit his lip, as if deciding something, then seemed to make up his mind. "I'm just gonna jump. Miley, before you go—I want to make sure you know how I feel about you."

Riiiing! Miley winced as her cell phone chose that moment to go off. Did Hannah have to get back already? She pulled the phone out of her purse and peered at the screen.

"Everything okay?" Travis asked.

No, it's definitely not! Miley thought. But all she said was, "I should take this. I'll just be a second, I swear." She slipped miserably out of her seat. "I bet I'll get better reception in back," she explained.

She raced out of the restaurant and back through the side door of the town hall. Then, after another quick change, she returned to the mayor's dinner dressed as Hannah.

"What did you tell them?" she asked Lilly as she took her seat beside her.

Before Lilly could answer, the mayor's wife leaned over. She patted Miley's stomach. "Sorry about your tummy," she said. "Happens to me when I travel, too."

"Yeah, thanks," Miley said. She rolled her eyes, then whispered to Lilly, "What was so important?!"

Lilly pointed at Miley's plate. A huge lobster was staring up at her. A waiter tied a lobster bib around her neck and the mayor announced, "Dig in!"

"So, Hannah," said Lorelai, who was sitting across the table. "You must have lots of wonderful stories."

"Not really," Miley replied, as her mind wandered back to Travis. Then she caught her dad's stern eye. "I mean . . . there are just so many. But I don't want tonight to be all about me," Miley went on. "Everyone's stories are important. Jackson, you just started college, right? Tell us about your classes."

"Uh, yeah, my classes," Jackson began.

He flashed a vengeful look at Miley.

"Yes, Jackson, tell us which is your favorite class, why don't you?" Mr. Stewart said, grinning.

And as Jackson groped for an answer, Miley stole away again.

Back at the restaurant, Miley sat down across from Travis and instantly sensed that something was wrong.

She looked down. Oh, no! She was still wearing the lobster bib!

"I'm having the lobster," she said.

Travis scanned the menu. "It's not on the menu," he said.

Miley winced, then took a deep breath to try to settle herself down. "Sorry," she said. "It's been a weird couple of days. But this . . . this is good." She gazed into Travis's eyes. "I think I know some of the things you want to tell me," she said. "And, to be honest, there are a lot of things I want to tell you, too. . . . But they're going to have to wait," she gasped as she suddenly spotted her father storming out of the town hall. "I'm going to double-check on those lobsters!"

Miley waited for her dad to give up looking for her and return inside . . . then she followed. After a quick change in the broom closet, she returned to the dining room—where Mr. Stewart was waiting.

"Sit!" he yelled, pointing to the table. "Enough! No one is getting up again! No one!" he said.

Miley sat down meekly as the guests exchanged uncomfortable glances.

"And, Jackson," he went on, "no more stories about a university you don't even attend!"

Jackson's mouth dropped open. "You . . . know?"

Mr. Stewart nodded. "Knew all along," he said.

Jackson glanced down the table at his cousin Derrick.

"Yup." Derrick nodded. "The whole petting-zoo gig—that was Uncle Robby's . . ."

". . . punishment," Mr. Stewart said.

"I'm sorry, Dad," gulped Jackson, not knowing what else to say. "I really . . ."

Lorelai tried to lighten the mood. "Dessert anyone?" she said. She signaled to a waiter, who pushed a cart into the room. "You've heard of Baked Alaska, well, we give you Tennessee Flambé!"

The waiter struck a match with a flourish and set the huge, meringue-covered dessert aflame.

"Mr. Mayor, I assume you'd like to say a

few final words," Lorelai added.

The mayor nodded . . . just as Cousin Derrick's ferret, Harlow, ran over and scurried up his leg!

All of a sudden, the mayor was yanking off his pants, Derrick was chasing after Harlow, the waiter was falling into the cart, and the flaming Tennessee Flambé was hurtling across the room.

Naturally, most of the guests saw a disaster. But Miley saw an opportunity. She dashed out and headed for the broom closet. Unfortunately, the cleaning lady was using the little room. But Miley didn't care. She grabbed her Hannah box and set off down the stairs.

As she pushed through the revolving glass door, Miley yanked off her Hannah wig and jewelry . . . then looked over to see not only her young fan, Cindy Lou, staring at her—but Travis, too!

"Travis," she called as he turned and began to walk away. "Let me explain."

"Explain what?" he asked, spinning around. "How you've been laughing at me? Making fun of me? Lying to me this whole time? I was honest with you. I told you how I felt."

"But I feel the same about you," she said.

"No, you don't," he replied. "Because I never would have treated you this way. You know what, just forget it, Miley . . . Hannah . . . whoever you are. We're done."

"Travis! Travis, wait!" she called. But he just stormed away.

Miley hung her head and slowly went back through the door. She couldn't even look at Cindy Lou. And she couldn't avoid her father.

"Did you see?" she asked when he met her by the stairs.

"Yeah, I saw," he said.

"Robby Ray?"

Miley and her dad both looked up. Lorelai was coming!

Mr. Stewart ran up the stairs to meet her. "Not now, Lorelai!" he said. "Got some family stuff goin' on."

Lorelai stopped.

"Sorry," he said. "There are some things going on with Miley. And with Hannah."

"Clearly," said Lorelai, frowning. "This evening was a disaster. I organized it, and that girl ruined it. I don't care if she is here to help."

"She has a complicated life," Mr. Stewart tried to explain.

Lorelai gave him a long look. "What's going on, Robby Ray?"

He wanted to answer her . . . but he didn't know how.

"You know what?" she went on. "I don't have much time for secrets and lies . . . and I don't think I could ever be happy with someone who's so comfortable livin' with 'em."

"And you shouldn't have to be," he responded. "I'm sorry for not telling you the truth. The truth is . . ." He paused. He wanted to be honest with Lorelai, but he just couldn't share Miley's secret. "I'm not in a place where I can be in a relationship," he said instead. "Miley and I . . . we need to sort some things out. She needs me, and I kinda gotta be there for her right now. I'm sorry."

Lorelai nodded. "Yeah. Me, too."

Miley listened from the steps below and couldn't keep from crying.

✳ ✳ ✳

Meanwhile, across the town square, Cindy Lou sat on a bench with her empty autograph book clutched in her hands. She was trying to make sense of all the strange things she'd seen, when an ice-cream cone suddenly appeared beside her.

"No luck, huh?" asked Oswald, this time dressed as an ice-cream man.

"No." The little girl sighed. "I saw her, though. A whole bunch of times. She kept going in and out the magic door — but she was always somebody different when she came out."

"Really?" Oswald's face lit up.

At last, the pieces of the Hannah puzzle were beginning to fit together.

Chapter Fourteen

The next day dawned gray and dreary—just like Miley's mood. But she went out in the rain anyway to try to work on her new song. When the showers stopped, her dad went out to find her.

"Hey," he said, stepping into the gazebo. He sat down beside her, and together they looked out across Grandma Ruby's farm. The sun was coming out, and everything looked fresh and green.

"You mad?" Miley asked at last, dreading the answer.

"Nah. Not mad," her father answered. "You?"

"No." She shook her head.

"How's the song coming?"

"I don't know," Miley said, sighing. "I'm not sure."

"What's it about?" he asked her.

"You. Me. Us." She shrugged. Then she went ahead and sang it.

"That's all I got," she said as the last note, full of feeling, faded away.

"It's good, Miley," her dad said. He held her close. "It's really good."

Then he nodded at her notebook, "So what else you got in there?"

Miley quickly closed it. "You'll see," she said. "Couple of things I've got to try and set right."

The next morning, Lilly found Miley asleep on top of the chicken coop. It had taken her all night, but she had finished it for Travis.

"Miley!" Lilly hollered, waking her with a start.

Miley tumbled off the roof and landed on a bale of hay.

"Is it time?" Miley asked, brushing the grass off her clothes.

Lilly grinned. "Yup. It's time."

A few hours later, people were streaming through Crowley Meadows toward a large, old stage. Excitement was in the air. The school orchestra was playing; vendors were selling food; there were even carnival rides and games. And much to Mr. Bradley's displeasure, the SAVE CROWLEY

MEADOWS udder sign was full!

Inside a lavish tour bus, Miley sat staring at her Hannah box. For the first time ever, she didn't want to open it.

Grandma Ruby sat beside her. "I know the gettin' here was hard," she told Miley. "But what you're doin' is a very good thing. You should be proud of that. I know I am." Then she took Miley's hand and laid a thin gold chain in it.

"This was Mom's," Miley said, recognizing the necklace.

"She'd be proud of you, too," Grandma Ruby told her.

She gave Miley a hug and helped her put the necklace on. Then she glanced out the bus window.

"Dang it," Grandma Ruby said as she caught Oswald trying to peek in. "No matter how much you scrape, some people just won't come off your shoe."

Vita quickly got some security guards to hustle him away. But Oswald didn't seem too bothered.

"I'm on to you, love," he told Vita smugly. "I've seen every person who's gotten on that bus. 'Course the real fun starts when we see who gets off." He grinned. "How's our little Hannah going to like that?"

"Why don't you ask her?" asked Vita. She nodded over his shoulder and Oswald followed her gaze. That blonde in the crowd—it was Hannah Montana!

"But how . . . ?" Oswald sputtered. "Hey! You! Come back. Somebody stop that pop star!"

Vita smiled as she watched him catch up to Hannah, only to discover it was Jackson in a wig!

"Hi," said Jackson. "Did you want to

buy a Hannah wig? All proceeds go to help save Crowley Meadows."

Jackson gestured to the dozens of blond heads among the crowd. Everywhere Oswald looked, in fact, he saw more Hannah Montanas!

"I don't like people messing with my Hannah," Vita said as she and Grandma Ruby walked up behind him.

"And nobody gets away with trying to hurt my Miley," Grandma Ruby added. "Now, I don't want any more trouble out of you, you hear?" she told Oswald. "No more sticking your nose into places it hasn't been invited. Destroying something that people love. Taking what's good and making it seem bad. I'm telling you right here, right now. I'm not gonna stand for it!"

Then suddenly the crowd rushed past

them toward the stage. The Hannah Montana concert was about to begin.

Finally, Hannah Montana was back onstage. But while her fans were as thrilled as ever, Miley wasn't. As she sang, she looked down at Lilly and her brother, at her grandma Ruby and her dad, and felt her heart grow heavy. They were always there for her . . . but could she say the same about herself? She saw Lorelai, too, off to the side, standing alone. Thanks to Miley, she hadn't spoken to Mr. Stewart—or Hannah—since the night before. And then she spotted Travis. She guessed he'd found the finished chicken coop . . . though she still couldn't believe he was at the concert.

Miley sang a few more lines, then stopped, very sad. "I can't do this," she said.

The band stopped playing, and the

people in the audience looked at each other, confused.

"I'm sorry," Miley told them. Then she shook her head. "You'd be amazed how many conversations I start that way. I've loved being Hannah," she went on. "But I don't think I can do it anymore. At least not here, not with you all. See, this is home. This is where I'm from. This is family. And there are only so many sacrifices you can ask a family to make." She paused to take a deep breath. "The last time I stood on this stage, I was six. I was just Miley." Then she reached up and pulled off her wig. "I still am."

Miley waited for the chorus of gasps to subside. "Hi. It's me. I've hurt a lot of people, but I didn't mean to," she went on. She locked eyes with Travis. "If it's not too late, I sure would like a second chance. I know you came to hear Hannah. But if you don't mind . . . I've written you all a song. It's kinda personal. A song about what I've learned over the last couple of weeks. Life's a climb," she said, smiling. "But the view's great."

Miley sang, and the whole audience, including Oswald, was spellbound. It was as if she were singing directly from her heart. When she finished, they cheered wildly and showered her with applause.

"Thanks for letting me live my Hannah," Miley told them. It had been fun, but now it was over. "Bye."

Then a small voice suddenly called out from the crowd: "Please be Hannah. We'll keep your secret."

Miley looked down to find Cindy Lou staring up at her with pleading eyes. Miley felt a tug at her heart, but she shook her head. "It's too late," she said. "I can't—"

"Sure you can!" Travis yelled.

Miley stared in disbelief. Had he really said that?

"Put the wig back on!" Vita called. "You'll never get to live a normal life if you don't."

"Nobody will tell," Lorelai added. "You came to help us. You're keeping us all together."

"Hannah's a part of you," shouted Lilly. "Don't let her go!"

Miley couldn't believe it. Even her dad was grinning and nodding. Hannah had messed up all their lives. How could they not want to let her go?

"Hannah! Hannah!" the crowd began to chant.

Miley was overwhelmed. She looked down at her Hannah wig and began to raise it to her head. Then she spotted Oswald taking pictures from offstage.

"No," Miley said. "Please . . ."

"Somebody stop him!" Lilly yelled.

That was Oswald's cue. He took off running. But Travis blocked him.

"Watch it," Oswald warned, as Miley's friends and family surrounded him. He held up his phone, which had Hannah's secret photos in it. "One more step and I hit send." He spoke into the phone. "I got the story, love. Photos and all."

Back in the offices of *Bon Chic*, Lucinda giggled, thrilled. "Oh, Ozzie, I never doubted you," she cooed. "What's the secret?"

Oswald hesitated.

"Don't do it, man," begged Mr. Stewart.

But Oswald shook his head. "Sorry, but there's nothing on Earth that could stop me from — "

"Daddy! Daddy!"

Oswald turned to see his daughters running toward him through the crowd.

"Phoebe, Clarissa—what are you doing here?" He gasped.

"This nice lady sorted it all out," Phoebe replied, pointing to Vita. "Two free tickets, first-class."

"Oh, I just thought the girls would appreciate a couple of free tickets. . . ." Vita grinned.

"Are we too late?" asked Clarissa. "We just got here. Is she going to sing again? Can we meet her?"

"I can't believe I'm one degree away from Hannah Montana!" Phoebe gushed. "Daddy, please," she begged. "I love Hannah!"

Torn, Oswald listened as Vita murmured in his ear: "Are you really going to destroy their dreams? Because that's what Hannah is all about. Is *that* your story?"

He looked at his girls and then at Miley as Vita's words sunk in. "No. That's not my story," he said at last. Then he picked up his phone again. "Lucinda, get this down. *Bon Chic* magazine is run by a wretchedly soulless succubus who preys upon the misfortune of others, and I am not going to put up with it any longer."

With an air of finality, Oswald closed his phone. "I think I just quit," he sighed.

Mr. Stewart patted him on the back as Vita led his daughters out to the front of the stage. "Something tells me Hannah has a few more songs in her," she told them.

In a moment, the only ones left backstage were Miley and Travis.

"So, what do you say, my Smiley Miley," he said as he took her hand. "Ready to get back up there and have some fun?"

She grinned. "I say, I think you're just as big a liar as I am," she teased. "You do too still have a crush on me!"

Travis laughed and gave Miley a kiss. A kiss that they had both been waiting a long time for.

Smiling, Miley turned and went to put her Hannah wig back on.

Moments later, Hannah strode back onstage and sang her latest song, "You'll Always Find Your Way Back Home."

The crowd went wild!

"Good night, y'all!" Hannah said when the song was over and the cheers and applause had quieted down. "Thanks for making this good ol' country girl's dreams come true!"